THE MATH INSPECTORS

BOOK ONE

The Case of the Claymore Diamond

Daniel Kenney & Emily Boever

BAKKEN
BOOKS

3rd Edition
ISBN: 9798327235663
Published by Bakken Books

BAKKEN
BOOKS

www.bakkenbooks.com

Table of Contents

1. September 9, 4:06 a.m.. 7

2. All Units Respond 10

3. A Strange Feeling 24

4. Three Problems 40

5. Numbers Never Lie 52

6. Situation Normal 62

7. The Wrong Guy...70

8. Stanley Robinson Carusoe 83

9. An Odds Solution 91

10. Stakeout 102

11. One Last Problem.. 111

12. MEANWHILE 120

13. BONUS MATH PROBLEMS............................... 123

HISTORIC
RAVENSBURG

Gertie **Felix** **Stanley** **Charlotte**
Hirschenbach Dervish Carusoe Miller

CHAPTER ONE

SEPTEMBER 9, 4:06 A.M.

A phone rang in a dark room, but the figure sitting nearby did not answer.

After a minute of silence, it rang again.

Same number.

A minute later, it rang yet again.

They would never stop calling.

The figure finally reached a trembling hand for the phone.

"Who is this?"

"Not the Boss, so this must be your lucky day," came the answer. "The Boss does not like to be kept waiting."

"I—I don't have the money."

A sigh crackled through the phone.

"I mean . . . I don't have it right now. I just need more time."

"Maybe you did not hear me," hissed the voice. "The Boss is not the waiting type."

"Just hear me out. I've got a plan, and I'll—I'll even pay an extra five percent on top of what I owe you!"

Cold silence filled the line.

The figure's heartbeat raced. This wasn't working. "Look, I used to know people who can move valuables on the black market, and—"

"The Boss knows all about your criminal past," said the voice. "As a matter of fact, I am looking at a file of rather impressive incriminating evidence against you right now. You need more time?"

"Yes."

"Well, this really must be your lucky day—you have one week to pull off your plan."

"You won't regret this!"

"We shall see," the voice said curtly. "But if you fail to deliver the money in one week, this file of evidence goes to the police, and I promise you, the only phone calls you'll be taking after that will be on the prison phone."

A trembling hand ended the call and turned on the light.

There was work to be done.

CHAPTER TWO

ALL UNITS RESPOND

This was Stanley Carusoe's New York. Not the steel-and-concrete jungle of Manhattan with its high-rises and low sewers and yellow taxis and dirty black streets. This was a spot two hours north of the city nestled between the Hudson River and the Catskill Mountains. A place filled with weird and wonderful people who ran businesses and raised families and hardly ever left. A place where girls and boys played and roamed and discovered and grew up. And a place where one particular 12-year-old boy with a great love for math and an even greater love for mystery was sitting in a tree house plotting his next adventure.

The place was called Ravensburg, and on this Saturday in September, the sticky heat of summer had momentarily stepped aside to make way for the slow, steady breezes of crystal-clear Canadian air. Stanley Carusoe sat up on the couch, peered out the window of the tree house, and smiled. A monarch butterfly danced in the wind on its long journey south. Change was in the air, Stanley thought.

Change was definitely in the air.

A noise pulled Stanley's attention away from the window. Gertie's round face popped up through the trapdoor.

"I hate her," she said.

"Hate who?" Felix asked, kneeling at the other tree house window and peering through a tiny pair of yellow binoculars.

Gertie stretched her neck. "Miss Perfect Polly Partridge. That's who."

"I know." Felix adjusted his binoculars slightly. "I just think it's funny to hear you say it. What'd she do to you this time?"

"You didn't see it? Well, she didn't just do it to *me*—she did it to *all* of us." Gertie climbed up, unzipped her backpack in the middle of the floor, and grumbling all the while, pulled something out.

Stanley knew she hadn't noticed him sitting on the couch. "What is that?"

Gertie jumped six inches and wheeled around. "Stanley Robinson Carusoe! Don't sneak up on me like that!" She blew dark bangs out of her eyes. "Here. Read for yourself."

Stanley grabbed the newspaper from Gertie, glanced at the headline, and frowned. "Um, Felix, you might want to take a look at this."

Felix shook his head. "Later, guys. I'm involved in a very important stakeout right now. Kinda life and death." Felix's tall, lanky frame was folded at odd angles, his elbows perched on the windowsill.

Gertie's eyes darted from the binoculars to the pile of candy wrappers on the floor, then back to Felix's usually freckled face. "Is that camouflage paint?" she asked Stanley. "What exactly is he doing?"

Stanley shrugged and handed the paper back.

"I'll tell you what I'm doing," Felix replied, still spying. "I left the last piece of my birthday cake on the kitchen counter so it can reach room temperature. Everybody knows it's mine, and everybody knows I'm waiting to have it tonight. Problem is, lately someone's been swiping my food, and nobody's fessed up to it. Well, not this time. I've got a perfect view of the kitchen from here, and this time," he shook his fist in the air, "I'm going to catch the thief red-handed."

Gertie put her hands on her hips and cocked her head a little to the left. "Life and death? That's not life and death, Felix. *This* is life and death." Her short stride kept pace with her temper as she crossed the tree house and poked the newspaper at his red head.

He ignored it. She looked down into the kitchen. "How long is your dumb stakeout going to take?"

"For your information, this isn't dumb, and it's not just any stakeout. It's a cake stakeout." He looked up and snapped his fingers. "Wait a second. That makes it a *cakeout!* Whoa. Anyway, I've been here for three hours, and I'm willing to wait thirty more to catch the culprit. In the past week, I've lost half a Twinkie, a piece of cinnamon toast, and leftover lasagna." After a pause, he turned to her for the first time. "Do you have any idea how good my mom's lasagna is on the second day?"

Stanley chuckled. If Felix was looking for sympathy, he wasn't going to find it with Gertie.

Felix returned to his binoculars.

"Have you even read yesterday's school newspaper?" Gertie practically screamed. "Polly wrote an editorial on 'Why English is the finest educational pursuit, followed by the arts, dance, science, and then,' get this, 'cleaning the bathroom and then math.' She cites studies that say people who like math are, quote: 'more likely to dress their pets up in sweaters, take stuffed animals with them to the movies, and lick paint off of houses.' End quote."

Felix jerked forward. "Why, that low-down—I can't believe it!"

"I know," Gertie said. "She's really gone too far this time."

"No, look. Something's happening in the house."

Stanley darted to the window. Even Gertie pushed onto her tiptoes to get a better view.

There was a blur of movement in the kitchen. Then something small and white jumped onto the counter. It was Buckets, the Dervish family's fluffy white cat. The fancy feline sniffed the edges of the birthday cake, licked the blue number 12 off the top, finished the entire piece in four bites, jumped down to the floor, and sauntered away.

The binoculars tipped from Felix's face. "That mangy, good-for-nothing cat burglar. See if I ever fill his milk bowl full again. And after everything I've done for him, everything we've meant to each other . . ."

Stanley patted him on the shoulder. "Sorry, buddy. I know how much that cake meant to you."

Gertie threw her hands in the air. "Cake? Who cares about cake? Look at this last sentence. 'The only people more pathetic than people who like math are the people in this school who act like math is their best friend.' *That* is a direct shot at *us*."

"I suppose it is." Felix sighed and started unwrapping another candy bar. "So, what do we do about it?"

He and Gertie both turned to Stanley.

But before Stanley could reply, the trapdoor flew open, and Charlotte came halfway up the ladder smiling at them. Her curly blond hair was drawn back in a ponytail, and her blue eyes sparkled with excitement.

Stanley looked down at her. "Did you get it?"

Charlotte heaved a cardboard box onto her shoulder. "Got it."

"Yeah, well, we've got something too," Gertie said, flailing her arm so violently that pieces of newspaper floated to the tree house floor. "A gigantic Polly Partridge problem. Why am I the only one upset by this whole thing?"

"Trust me, Gertie," Stanley said. "You're not." He reached down to lift the box up the ladder. "Polly will get what's coming to her." He took something out of the box—an electronic device with lots of knobs—and set it on the small table near the middle of the clubhouse. "But not today. Today, we have better things to do." He held up a black power cord coming off the end of the device. "Today, we discover our destiny."

Gertie eyed the outlet at the other end of the tree house. "It looks like our destiny needs an extension cord. What is that thing, anyway?"

Stanley nodded toward the trunk. "Get the extension cord and I'll show you."

Gertie bowed. "Whatever you say, dear leader. But don't think I've forgotten about Polly."

Charlotte pulled herself into the tree house, leaned over the gadget, and tapped on it. "I haven't tried this thing yet. Not even sure if it still works." She looked up at Felix. "Nice camo, by the way."

"Not much good it did me," Felix mumbled, his mouth full of Snickers.

"Take it you don't need these after all?" Charlotte unslung a pair of high-powered hunting binoculars from around her neck.

"Nah, Operation Cake Bait couldn't wait. Thanks for bringing them, but my little Happy Meal Spynoculars worked just as well."

"Culprit?" Charlotte asked.

"Buckets," Felix answered.

"Bummer," Charlotte replied. She looked over at Gertie. "Cats eat cake?"

Gertie smirked. "Cats? No. Buckets? Anything."

"It's always been a source of bonding." Felix sighed. "Until now."

Stanley plugged the device into the extension cord. "Felix, see if you can get this thing to work."

"If it's electronic, I'll get it to work," Felix said. He ran his fingers over the strange device.

"This had better be some sort of getting-even machine, Stanley," Gertie said.

Felix switched the power to the *on* position and adjusted a lever. He shook his head, then pulled a screwdriver out of his pocket and stuck it into the machine next to the lever. He leaned forward, then smiled. "It's alive."

They all held their breath and leaned in. Voices started crackling to life.

"A radio?" Gertie asked.

"It's an old police scanner," Charlotte replied. "We found it up in my attic, and Mr. Big Ideas here thought we needed it in the tree house. I once saw the guys on *MythBusters* try to toast bread with one. You know, in case of an emergency."

"In case you need to toast bread while fighting crime?" Felix scratched his chin. "I like it."

Charlotte shrugged. "Yeah, well, don't get your hopes up. It didn't work."

"And how *exactly* is this our destiny, Stanley?" Gertie asked.

"Well, I *do* love toast," Felix suggested.

"No toast," Stanley said. "Forget the toast. We're going to listen in on police chatter. When a crime has been committed, they talk about it on the radio. We listen, then go to the scene to watch the police in action. And I thought maybe we could . . . you know, even help solve a crime . . . or two."

There was a long moment of silence.

"You want to start a detective agency?" Gertie asked.

"Well, I don't know." Stanley stuffed his hands in his pockets. "I just thought we would have fun."

"Are you kidding?" Felix said. "We'd be just like those meddlesome kids on *Scooby-Doo!* Solving mysteries, foiling plots, catching bad guys, and all while wearing groovy scarves. When do we start, gang?"

Charlotte punched Felix in the shoulder. "Thought I told you the cartoon thing was weird."

"Zoinks!" Felix said, rubbing his arm.

Gertie leaned down for a closer look at the police scanner. "Okay, it *is* a cool idea. Except for the scarf thing." She looked up at Stanley. "But you promise we'll get Polly back?"

Stanley drew his right forefinger across his chest twice. "Cross my heart."

The friends crowded around, and Stanley turned up the volume. For the next two hours, they planned their new club (very exciting) and listened to police chatter (not terribly exciting).

The radio reported on someone with too many unpaid parking tickets.

"Let's call ourselves the Math Bandits."

"Yes, that would be a great name. If we were criminals!"

Somebody was driving with a broken taillight.

"I've got it—the Anti-English Club."

"Well, it's better than the Anti-Criminal Mathter Minds!"

A cat (not Buckets—though Felix was hopeful) was reportedly stuck up a tree.

"A slushie fund?"

"All I'm saying is, we'll need a lot of snacks. And probably matching uniforms."

They were just discussing meeting up again after dinner when something new buzzed through the scanner. The voice was surprisingly calm for such big news.

"Armed robbery at 429 Main Street, Franklin's Jewelry. Suspect has fled the scene and may be armed. Proceed with caution. All units respond. All units respond."

The four friends stared at each other for a moment. Then all at once, they scrambled for the trapdoor, bolted down the ladder, untangled their bikes, and sped off.

CHAPTER THREE
A STRANGE FEELING

The Historic District of Ravensburg was exactly three blocks long. The oldest part of town, it was made up of brick streets, picturesque buildings, old trees, and colorful flowers. Normally, the mile ride from Felix's house would have taken only a few minutes. But on this day, news traveled faster than bikes, and the onlookers heading to Franklin's Jewelry Store delayed the four friends.

Police cruisers were parked at odd angles along Main Street, and an officer was already stringing yellow tape in a semicircle around Franklin's in an effort to keep the steadily growing crowd at a distance. Behind him, an older man sat on the edge of a stretcher holding an ice pack to his bandaged, bloody head.

At the center of the commotion, Police Chief Abrams bent over a map laid out on the hood of a police car. Several officers were crowded around him. "If Franklin's is here," Abrams was saying, jabbing at the map, "then we need roadblocks set up at a 30-mile radius on all major routes."

"Chief," a young officer interrupted, "do we have the manpower for that?"

"No, I want the state patrol in on this. In fact, I'll bring in the park rangers if I have to. We just had a felony assault on a respected citizen, plus the theft of the Claymore Diamond. I was brought in as chief to clean up this town, and that's just what I'm going to do. One crime at a time. We need to find whoever did this, and fast—or heads are going to roll."

Stanley turned to the others. "Did you hear that?"

"I know," Gertie snorted. "Could he have squeezed one more cliché into that little speech?"

"I mean about the Claymore Diamond. That's gotta be worth like—"

Felix held up his phone and showed them the results of his internet search. "Like $100,000, according to insurance value."

Charlotte whistled. "That's a lot of dough."

"No joke," Felix said. "And look what they did to Old Man Franklin."

Gertie shook her head at Felix. "*Old Man Franklin?*"

"Have you guys never seen a single *Scooby-Doo* episode? There's always an Old Man Somebody who gets robbed."

"Shall we just pull off the culprit's mask now and be done with the mystery, Shaggy?" Gertie said.

"If only it were that easy in real life," Felix said.

"Come on," Stanley said. "Let's find out what's going on."

The kids dropped their bikes next to a light pole and snaked their way through the crowd. On the far side of the crime scene, they spotted an officer writing notes on a pad. Officer Bobby Evans—the kids knew him well from his prior assignment as a school resource officer. They skirted along the edge of the police tape to get closer to him.

Evans looked up as the kids approached. "Hey, kids. What are you guys up to? Staying out of trouble?"

"No," Gertie said. "We're here to confess to stealing the Claymore Diamond."

Evans stared at them.

Stanley chuckled. He knew that Gertie and Evans sometimes butted heads. "We overheard the chief talking. Too bad about Mr. Franklin. Is he going to be all right?"

"Should be," Evans said, "though he took a nasty blow to the head."

"Can you tell us what happened?" Felix asked. "We've started a detective agency. You know, 'The

Mathkateers—You Can Count on Us, and We Can . . . um . . . Count.'"

Charlotte jabbed an elbow at Felix. "We haven't settled on an official name yet, or a motto. But give us a try. Maybe we could help."

Felix moved closer to Evans. "Name or not, we're colleagues now. So, what's the inside scoop?"

"Colleagues, huh?" The corner of Evans's mouth angled slightly. "Then why don't you tell me what *you* think happened here?"

"It might help if I could see the crime scene up close," Stanley said.

Officer Evans waved his hand once. Stanley grabbed Gertie's notepad, stepped under the tape, and crossed through the police barrier.

"The things I do for you kids," the young officer said. He pointed at the store's front step. "Sit right there and don't touch anything."

Stanley surveyed the scene. Mr. Franklin being loaded into the ambulance. Glass on the sidewalk

outside the broken storefront window. Thick tire marks lining the street in front of them. Stanley opened Gertie's notebook. "I need to see it all on paper. Helps me think."

"It's clear as day what happened here," Felix said. "Aliens. Old Man Franklin's just lucky they were after the Claymore Diamond and not him."

Officer Evans rolled his eyes. "Obviously."

"Okay," Stanley said. "I'll take a stab at it. From what I can tell, Mr. Franklin was in the store when it was robbed, and he put up a fight. He lost. The glass on the ground outside means the window was broken from the inside. And by the looks of the skid marks, the robber jumped into his car and sped out of here in a hurry."

Evans's mouth curled into a half grin. "Not bad. Well, I suppose there's no harm in filling you in on a few things. It'll all be public news in about ten minutes anyway, judging by the media van that just pulled up."

He looked down at his notes. "According to Mr. Franklin, a white male in his mid-twenties by the name of Christopher Anderson came into the store just a little before closing. Mr. Anderson and Mr. Franklin got into an argument." He flipped a page on his notepad. "Then Mr. Anderson grabbed a paperweight and cracked Mr. Franklin on the head. The 911 call came in from Mrs. Sheila Blump—she owns the store next to Franklin's—and when Mr. Franklin woke up in a pool of his own blood a few minutes later, he noticed that his display case had been smashed and two diamond rings had been taken. Then he saw that his Lock Pro 2000 was open—um, that's the model of Franklin's safe—and his most prized possession, the Claymore Diamond, was gone."

At that moment, Evans's radio crackled. "Suspect Christopher Anderson is in custody. Repeat, suspect in custody. Got him at the junction of Highways 50 and 6."

Chief Abrams's voice bellowed through the radio. "Good work. Did he give you any problems?"

"No, Chief," came the answer. "No problems at all. We got him at the roadblock. Routine stop."

Stanley saw Charlotte look at her watch. She was a stickler for detail.

"They *got* him," Evans said. "Thankfully, that didn't take too long. Maybe I can still catch the game tonight."

The voice came through the radio again. "Hey, Chief, turns out we do have a problem. No Claymore

Diamond, no diamonds of any kind, and Anderson isn't talking. He must've stashed them someplace."

Chief Abrams's voice rumbled. "Start a search of the area now! Nobody goes home until we find that diamond."

Evans sighed. "Looks like that game will have to wait."

"I bet we could help," Stanley suggested. "We *are* pretty smart."

Evans laughed. "Nice seeing you kids, but it's time to let the pros handle this."

Stanley had a thought. "Hey—when you're done, do you think we could get a copy of the official police report? It would be helpful for us to see how real police officers do their jobs."

Evans shook his head. "No can do, Stanley. That file is official police business. Like I said, you kids run along home." He returned his attention to his notebook and walked away. "And be good," he said over his shoulder, looking right at Gertie.

She curtsied and flashed a fake smile.

"Stanley, what's on your mind?" Charlotte said. "I know that look. They got the guy, so why do you want the police report?"

"You heard him. Until they find the diamond, the case isn't closed. What if Anderson had an accomplice? Let's snoop around and see what we come up with."

"How exactly does one snoop?" Felix asked.

"A real *Scooby-Doo* fan would never have to ask that question," Stanley said. "Just do what you're good at."

And that's what they did. Gertie took out her pen and paper and wrote down everything she saw and heard. Charlotte climbed a tree and snapped mental pictures of the scene. Felix took out his camouflage handkerchief, hung it around his neck, leaned up against a tree, and said, "Groovy."

And Stanley looked around for Sheila Blump, the owner of the store next door. But before he could find her, a familiar voice rose above the noise of the crowd.

"This is Stella Burger reporting live from Franklin's Jewelry Store, where Ravensburg's most respected precious metals establishment has been robbed. That's right, Dan. I said robbed!"

She's talking to Dan Flounder back in the studio, Stanley thought.

The reporter was clutching Mrs. Blump by the arm just out of camera shot. Now Stella yanked the heavyset woman into view.

"As usual, we are breaking news here at Channel 12. I have with me Mrs. Sheila Blump, owner of Blump's Blooms and Bonbons, who has been Mr. Franklin's closest neighbor on Main Street for years. Mrs. Blump, tell us what you know." Stella thrust the microphone in Mrs. Blump's face.

Mrs. Blump, it turned out, didn't need further prompting. "Well, I'll tell you all about my experience, Stella. I was minding my own business, literally. I mean I was just putting the finishing touches on some chocolate truffles—" She grabbed the microphone and leaned forward. "Which are all buy-one-get-one-half-off the rest of the day in solidarity with poor Mr. Franklin—when I saw Christopher Anderson walk into Mr. Franklin's store at exactly 5:55 p.m. All of a sudden, I heard this terrific commotion. Now, I'm not one for meddling in other people's affairs—just ask anyone—but I couldn't help but overhear."

"And what is it that you heard?" Stella asked, grabbing the microphone back.

"Shouting. Yes, indeed. I heard shouting, though at first, I couldn't make out what they were saying. Then someone screamed, 'You're a liar and a thief, and you'll never get away with this!' Then it sounded like they were wrestling or something. Next thing I knew, there was this big crash, and that Anderson guy went running out of the store, jumped into his car, and sped off. Well, I have several years of parks-and-recreation judo training under my belt, so I knew my duty. I ran right over there, and when I saw dear old Mr. Franklin on the floor, I made the call to the police and stood guard until they came to relieve me. The whole thing has been so upsetting."

Stella angled the microphone back. "I can't imagine, Mrs. Blump. You're so brave. And we'll all sleep better tonight knowing an alleged felon is off the streets. Incidentally, how do you know it was Christopher Anderson you saw?"

"Well," Mrs. Blump said, "I didn't know his name until today when the police said they were hunting him, but I recognized his face. He's been coming to Franklin's on the 15th of every month for a while now. And when he's done, he always comes into my place and buys a dozen chocolate truffles—which are all buy-one-get-one-half-off this whole week. To think, all these months, I've been gift-wrapping bonbons for a hooligan."

Stella Burger looked directly into the camera with an enormous toothy smile. "The police have confirmed for us that Christopher Anderson is in custody, although the Claymore Diamond is still missing. I repeat, the diamond is still missing. But I'm on this story for you, Ravensburg, so keep it tuned here for more news as it happens. Reporting live from Franklin's Jewelry Store, I'm Stella Burger from Action 12 News. Remember, '12 is Swell.' Back to you, Dan."

Gertie opened her mouth so wide, Stanley thought she might swallow her own face. Then she did a spot-on impersonation of Stella Burger. "Remember, '12 is Swell!' Seriously, it doesn't even rhyme!"

The crowd began to break up, and a young policewoman escorted Mrs. Blump away. *Probably wasn't supposed to be talking to the media,* Stanley thought. Now he wouldn't be able to ask her any questions either.

He and Gertie headed back to their bikes, where Felix and Charlotte were waiting.

"Anything to report?" Stanley asked.

"Not sure what's important," Charlotte said, "but I looked at everything I could."

"And I've got half a notepad full," Gertie said.

They all turned to Felix.

"Oh, yeah," he said. "I've got plenty. Where do I even begin to explain what's in here right now?" He tapped the side of his head. "Lots. Maybe too much."

Gertie rolled her eyes.

"What about you, Stanley?" Charlotte asked.

"I don't know, guys," Stanley said. "I've got a strange feeling about this."

Charlotte shot Gertie a look, and they both giggled. "You mean you've got a Stanley?"

Stanley scrunched his face up. "Huh?"

"We decided to call a funny feeling a *Stanley*," Charlotte explained.

"On account of you having funny feelings so much," Gertie said.

"Yeah, dude," Felix said. "We're basically making fun of you."

"Thank you, Felix. I gathered that. And I can't help it, but I do get funny feelings."

"You mean *Stanleys*," Felix reminded him.

"And I say we meet at the tree house tomorrow morning and review everything we know. I think the police may be missing something."

CHAPTER FOUR
THREE PROBLEMS

Gertie, Felix, and Charlotte were already in the tree house the next morning when Stanley climbed through the trapdoor. They were crowded around the television.

"What are you guys watching?"

Felix took a break from munching on popcorn. "Chief Abrams is holding a press conference with the district attorney. Get over here."

Stanley sat on the arm of the couch with a manila folder in his hand.

On screen, Abrams was just finishing up. "And because of this, the district attorney has agreed not only to charge Mr. Anderson with grand theft larceny, but also with felony assault. It's only a matter of time until we find the Claymore Diamond, but until then, we've already got enough evidence to take this to trial."

"Well," Gertie said, "I guess we're sleuths without a case. Any chance Polly Partridge needs some embarrassing secrets detected?"

The station went to commercial, and Stanley reached down to turn off the TV.

"Wait a minute," Felix said. "I wanna watch this. It's a commercial for next week's heavyweight boxing match." He cupped his hands and boomed like an announcer, "And in this corner, the heavyweight champion of the world, Vladimir Levchin!" Then he shrugged. "It may not be pro wrestling, but it's still gonna be fun."

Stanley shook his head and turned off the TV. "Guys, this is serious. Chief Abrams is getting way ahead of himself. Come here and take a look at this." He opened his folder on the table, and they all huddled around.

"I was up forever last night trying to figure out what was bothering me. Then I realized there were three big problems, but I need you guys to help me verify a few things."

"Only three problems?" Charlotte teased.

"Let's have the first one," Gertie said.

Stanley handed them each a piece of paper. "I've put together a timeline of events comparing the information we heard from Officer Evans and Mrs. Blump."

"You're saying they're different?" Felix asked.

"Actually, we'll get to that later. But first, there's the matter of the safe. Stay with me here. Franklin told the police that when he came to consciousness, the safe was open. But here's the problem. Evans said the safe was a Lock Pro 2000. I looked up that model online, and it's got four different tumblers, almost like a bike combination lock. At first glance, it seems kind of simple, like maybe you'd be able to guess the combination. But then I took a closer look at the math.

"Each of the four tumblers of the Lock Pro 2000 has the numbers 0 through 9. In order to open the safe, each tumbler has to be on the exact right number. Felix, double-check my math. What are the odds of Anderson guessing the right combination?"

Felix scratched his chin. "Well, to figure out how many possible combinations there are, you examine the possible number of digits for each tumbler and then multiply them. Each of the four tumblers would have 10 possibilities, so you take 10 x 10 x 10 x 10, which is . . . 10,000."

"So, ten thousand different possible combinations?" Charlotte shook her head. "He'd have to be the luckiest guy in the world. It would take forever to try all of them."

Gertie wrote something in her notepad, then looked up. "So, you're saying Anderson discovered the combination ahead of time?"

"Or," Stanley said, "Franklin *told* him the combination. But neither Evans nor Blump said anything about that."

"What if he was a master safecracker?" Felix suggested. "You know, like in the movies where they use a stethoscope to listen to the clicks inside the lock?"

Stanley nodded. "Maybe. We don't know. And until we do, that's problem number one."

"Problem number one, the safe," Gertie said, writing that down. "Okay, give us number two."

"Well, Mrs. Blump said she saw Anderson go into Franklin's at exactly 5:55 p.m." Stanley paused and let his friends study the timeline.

Gertie flipped through her notes, then slapped her hand on the table. "The timeline doesn't work, does it?"

"Nope," Stanley said. "We were there talking to Officer Evans when he got the call that Anderson was taken into custody. Charlotte, what was the exact time?"

"The call came in at 6:21 p.m."

"The beauty of a photographic memory," Felix said. "Want to put your superpowers to work nabbing a thieving cat when this is all over?"

As usual, the others ignored Felix's antics. "Just think about everything that would need to have happened," Stanley continued. "At 5:55 an argument, then a fight, then the display case breaks, the window gets busted, and Mrs. Blump calls the cops. Before they arrive, Anderson somehow cracks the safe. Then he stashes the Claymore Diamond somewhere and makes it out to Highways 50 and 6 by 6:21. I don't think he could pull all that off in 25 minutes."

"Twenty-six minutes, actually," Charlotte corrected. "But I see your point. Let's run it through."

"Okay," Stanley said, rising from his seat and pacing around the tree house. "So, Anderson comes in at 5:55 p.m. He and Franklin argue, the window is broken, and he hits Franklin over the head. Then Anderson busts the diamond cases, grabs some rings, and goes to the safe. How long would it take to do all of that *and* crack the safe?"

"I don't know," Felix said. "Ten minutes if he knows the combination or is a crackerjack safecracker. All night if he was guessing the combination."

"And since he did get into the safe, let's assume he didn't guess. So, let's go with ten minutes. That means at the earliest, Anderson leaves the jewelry store at 6:05. That gives him 16 minutes to get to the corner of Highway 50 and Highway 6. Felix, how many miles from the jewelry store to that intersection?"

Felix punched the information into his tablet and searched. "26.3 miles."

"And could he travel 26.3 miles in 16 minutes?" Stanley asked.

Felix gestured to Gertie. "It's Gertie time," he said.

Gertie was already scribbling. "So, if he had to go 26.3 miles in 16 minutes, then to figure out how far he traveled in one minute, I divide 26.3 by 16. And I get . . . hmmmm . . . 1.64 miles per minute."

"Good," Stanley said. "Now convert that to miles per hour."

"Already happening. Since there are 60 minutes in an hour, I multiply 1.64 miles per minute by 60 minutes, and that gives me . . ." Gertie looked confused. "Something's not right, Stanley." She chewed on her pencil. "Not with my math, I mean. That's perfect. With your numbers."

"Just give us the answer."

"Well, it says here that in order for Anderson to get out to Highways 50 and 6 by 6:21, he would need to travel 98 miles per hour."

"Wow!" Felix said. "That's really fast."

"Yep," Stanley agreed. "Way *too* fast. And remember, Anderson also had to stash the stolen goods on the way, so he would have needed to go even faster. But remember the call Officer Evans got?"

Charlotte spoke up. "'No problems at all,' they said. 'We got him at the roadblock. Routine stop.'"

Stanley smiled. "Exactly. If Anderson was driving over 100 miles per hour, don't you think the officer who stopped him would have mentioned that?"

Felix shook his head. "You're right—the timeline doesn't make sense. Mrs. Blump saw Anderson go in at 5:55, so Anderson was definitely there. But there's no way he would have had enough time to do all that stuff and get to that roadblock by 6:20."

"6:21," Charlotte corrected.

Felix tipped an invisible hat to her. "6:21."

"Okay," Gertie said, counting on her fingers. "So, getting into Franklin's safe is a problem, and the timeline is a problem. What else? You said you had three things, so what's the third?"

"I think Mrs. Blump knows more than she said yesterday."

Felix folded his arms. "Just what are you suggesting?"

"I've got a . . . well, I've got a *Stanley* that Mrs. Blump is lying."

"No way," Felix said. "There is no way a chocolate artist like her is lying. That woman is part angel. I stand with Blump."

Stanley shook his head. "Sorry, Felix. But this timeline problem is irrefutable. Her statement that Anderson came in at 'exactly 5:55 p.m.' just can't be right. Plus, I went by her place this morning, and I've never seen it so packed. She's doing awfully well with this publicity. I think you and Gertie should go down there today and talk to her. See if you can dig anything else up."

"You want me to go down to Blump's? I knew I was going to love this detective stuff," Felix said. "What are we looking for—besides half-priced 'Franklin truffles'? They're on sale all week, you know."

"Try to ask her questions about what happened," Stanley said. "Don't press her too hard—you don't want her to get suspicious—but she'll probably want to talk, even if the cops have asked her not to. And while you guys are doing that, Charlotte and I can go to the hospital to see if we can talk to Mr. Franklin. Sound like a plan?"

Everyone nodded.

"I just wish we could talk to Mr. Anderson," Charlotte said. "From what the chief said today before you showed up, Anderson hasn't said a word since they nabbed him."

"Maybe Mr. Anderson thinks he can make some kind of deal with the cops if he delays telling them where the diamond is," Gertie suggested. "That sort of thing always works on TV."

"Hmm, maybe," Stanley said. "Anyway, keep your eyes peeled for numbers. If we find the right numbers, we find the truth."

CHAPTER FIVE
NUMBERS NEVER LIE

Stanley and Charlotte made their way to the maternity ward of Ravensburg Mercy Hospital and sat down in the waiting room. A nervous grandfather-to-be rocked back and forth as his wife snored on the seat next to him. A minute later, his eyes started to close too.

Looks like it's been a long night, Stanley thought.

A pretty nurse in her mid-forties came in, her pink scrubs contrasting sharply with her chocolate-brown skin. The snoozing man startled as she passed, jumped up, and threw confetti. The nurse shielded her head too late, and most of it landed right in her face.

"Not yet, Mr. Firnmeyer. But soon. I'll go get the vacuum. Again." She noticed the kids. "Stanley? Charlotte? What are you doing here?"

Charlotte gave a little wave. "Hi, Mrs. C."

Stanley pushed his glasses up the bridge of his nose. "We're looking for some help, Mom."

Stanley's mom rolled her eyes. "Leave me out of it, Stanley. Here, follow me. I've got to get this stuff out of my hair."

"Leave you out of what?" Stanley said.

"Whatever mischief you're up to." Mrs. Carusoe punched in some numbers on a keypad and opened a heavy door that read *Hospital Staff and Registered Visitors Only.*

"Mom, did you hear about what happened to Mr. Franklin last night?"

"Yes, poor man. He was brought here for treatment."

"Do you think you could get me in to talk to him?"

Stanley's mom put her hands on her hips and looked over her glasses at him. "Why?"

"Just curious."

"Stanley Robinson Carusoe, you are never *just* curious. You're always up to something. Besides, what makes you think that poor man wants to talk to a couple of kids after all he went through yesterday?"

"Because, Mom." Stanley smiled. "Kids make everything better."

His mom rolled her eyes again.

Stanley folded his hands. "Please? I'll clean the whole house before you get home."

She stopped, turned slowly, and studied him. "*Really* clean? Like, even the laundry?"

"Even the laundry. Promise."

They had just reached the nurses' station. Stanley's mom pursed her lips for a minute. Then she walked behind the counter, looked at the computer screen, and made a few mouse clicks. "Okay, I'm due for a break. I'll take you up to his room, but no guarantees that he'll want to see you. Understand?"

"Thanks, Mom."

"Just let me get this confetti out of my hair first. You kids wait here. I'll be right back."

As soon as she left, Charlotte turned to Stanley. "Your mom is right. Why would Franklin want to see a couple of kids?"

Stanley rubbed his chin. "I'm working on that."

Stanley's mom returned a minute later. There was still some confetti in her hair, but not as bad as before. She led them to the elevator, and as they rode up to the fourth floor, she looked down at Charlotte. "How did you let Stanley rope you into another one of his schemes?"

Charlotte shrugged. "Not sure you've noticed, Mrs. C., but Stanley can be a real pain—I mean, a little persistent sometimes. Even if his ideas can be a bit crazy."

Stanley's mom laughed. "I always did like you, Charlotte."

The elevator opened, and they walked to Mr. Franklin's room. Stanley's mom stopped them just short of the door. "He'll want to know why you're here to see him."

"Just tell him we want to learn about how Mr. Anderson cracked open his safe."

She gave Stanley a funny look, but she slipped into Mr. Franklin's room without asking for an explanation.

Less than a minute later, she came back out with an even funnier look on her face. "I don't know how you do it, but Mr. Franklin said he'll see you now. I'd better get back to work. But don't stay in there long, you hear? He's still pretty worn out."

"Thanks, Mom. Really."

As she walked away down the hall, Mrs. Carusoe hollered, "Even the laundry, Stanley. Even the laundry!"

Stanley pushed open the door to Mr. Franklin's room, and Charlotte followed him inside.

Mr. Franklin sat on the side of his hospital bed wearing normal clothes. He pointed at two chairs. "Your mom said you wanted to come visit me. How very nice of you. As you can see, I'm about to be released." He was leaning on his cane, and the edges of his mouth looked like they hurt. "What can I do for you? You wanted to know something about my safe?"

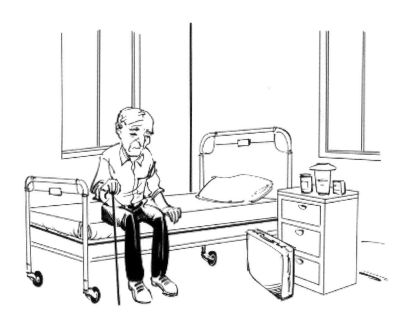

"We're so sorry for what happened to you, Mr. Franklin," Stanley said. "And I'm sorry to bother you, really, but my friends and I like to solve puzzles, and I was curious about something." He rubbed his palms together. "That guy, Mr. Anderson—did he ask you for the combination to your safe?"

Mr. Franklin shook his head and looked steadily at Stanley. "Not that I recall."

Charlotte leaned forward in her chair. "So, that means he cracked the safe?"

Franklin shook his head again, shifting his gaze to Charlotte. "I don't know what he did, young lady. At the time, I was knocked out silly on the floor. As I told the police, Mr. Anderson became angry, we got into a fight, the window broke, and he hit me over the head. Everything went dark, and the next thing I knew, I was waking up, the safe was open, and the Claymore Diamond was gone."

Just then a nurse came into the room, looked sideways at Charlotte and Stanley, and put on a pair of latex gloves. "Before you leave, Mr. Franklin, I need to check your injury again."

Stanley had one more question. "Do you remember what time Mr. Anderson came into your store?"

Franklin twisted his cane nervously and shook his head. "Sorry, I don't."

The nurse gently removed his bandages and examined his head. "This is going to heal up quickly. I still can't believe how straight the cut is." She squinted. "Cleanest head injury I've seen in my 17 years as a nurse, I can tell you that. You might not feel like it now, Mr. Franklin, but you're very lucky. It could have been a lot worse."

"I guess the odds were in my favor for once." Mr. Franklin laughed.

The nurse applied new bandages, took off her gloves, and smiled. "Okay, Mr. Franklin, consider yourself officially discharged. Let me help you out." She reached down to pick up the old man's briefcase, but he snatched it from her.

"Thank you, but I'm not so bad off that I can't get my own things." He slung his jacket over one arm, donned his hat, and turned to the kids with a smile. "I do appreciate you coming to visit me, but I guess they're kicking me out."

Mr. Franklin walked somewhat unsteadily into the hallway, clutching his briefcase with one hand and the nurse's arm with the other. Stanley and Charlotte followed them down the corridor and rode down with them on the elevator, but they didn't ask him any more questions. Several reporters were waiting for Mr. Franklin at the exit, but he climbed into a cab and rode away without saying a word.

Charlotte and Stanley headed to their bikes.

"What do you make of him?" Charlotte asked.

Stanley held up one hand while he took out his phone with the other. He looked up the number he wanted, then dialed. As the phone rang, he covered it and said, "I've got to get that house clean, but we don't have time."

A voice answered. "Rita's Cleaning Service."

"Rita?" Stanley said. "Stanley Carusoe. I need that favor now—like, this afternoon. Any chance you can fit me in? Perfect. My house. Yep, the whole thing. Oh, and Rita, the laundry too. You're the best. Thanks!" He hung up.

Charlotte looked at him in disbelief. "How did you manage that?"

"I did Rita's taxes last year. Saved her business a bundle of money."

Charlotte chuckled. "Whose taxes *haven't* you done? So, what did you think about Mr. Franklin?"

"Call it a funny . . . well, you know, but I'm placing Mr. Franklin on my Blump list. He's saying less than he knows."

"Or maybe he's an old man who got knocked on the head and is really confused?"

"Maybe. I don't know. People are confusing, but numbers *aren't* confusing. And right now, I really need some numbers."

CHAPTER SIX
SITUATION NORMAL

The four friends met at Mabel's Diner to discuss their investigation. Stanley and Charlotte had just finished reporting on their hospital visit when the chocolate milkshakes arrived. Felix's, as usual, was Mondo-sized.

Gertie looked at him with exasperation.

"What? I'm trying to put on some weight," he explained. "It's so hard."

Gertie squinted her eyes at him as she touched her chubby cheeks. "Yes, I don't know how you bear it. I do hate you, Felix Dervish. You know that, right?"

"Hey, you act like I *wanna* feel this hungry all the time."

Stanley laughed. "Well, Shaggy," he said, "what did you learn?"

"As I suspected, Mrs. Blump has been completely exonerated," Felix said, slurping his milkshake so loudly that people around the diner looked their way.

Gertie shook her head and looked at Stanley. "I don't know which Sheila Blump he was listening to, but the one *I* talked to likes to stretch her stories longer than her saltwater taffy. You were right, Stanley. She was pretending not to be," Gertie made air quotes with her fingers, "*at liberty* to talk about *her experience,* and then she spent 20 minutes dragging us through every detail. She's keeping with the 5:55 timeframe, but other things have already changed from yesterday. I swear she kept describing the order of what happened differently each time she said it."

"Anything stand out in particular?" Stanley asked.

"The buy-one-get-one-half-off Franklin truffles were outstanding," Felix offered.

"Actually," Gertie said, "the bottomless pit next to you may be on to something there. Sheila is making a killing with all this publicity. Get this. She has the gift-wrapped truffles she *says* she made up for Mr. Anderson—you know, the ones he never picked up—

under glass. She's going to auction them off to the highest bidder tomorrow."

"What do you mean, she *says* those are the ones she wrapped for Mr. Anderson?" Charlotte asked. "Don't you believe her?"

"Well, you should see this thing. It's all in gold paper and has this beautiful bow on top. It's just so funny to think of a criminal ordering something so . . . girly. So, I asked if that was the same thing he bought on his monthly visits. Blump said no, that Mr. Anderson ordered this month's box of truffles twice as big as usual, and she didn't see a thing wrong with auctioning it off for a little money." Gertie looked down at her notepad. "Otherwise, Blump said Mr. Anderson was polite and quiet and always paid in cash. Not sure if paying in cash means anything, but I thought it was worth noting."

"I'm not sure either," Stanley said. He tipped his milkshake glass upside down and tapped the last few drops into his mouth. "I'm not sure about anything.

Maybe Mr. Anderson *is* the bad guy after all, Mr. Franklin is only a scared old man, and Sheila Blump is nothing more than a money-grubbing busybody. All we know for sure is that Sheila Blump and Mr. Franklin didn't clear up any of our three problems for us. And we're out of leads."

"And I'm off to the bathroom," Charlotte said, scooting out of the booth.

Gertie clinked her spoon against her milkshake glass and smiled at Stanley. "I suppose crime scene photos wouldn't help, would they?"

Stanley's mood changed instantly. "No way. You got photos? How'd you worm your way into the jewelry store?"

Gertie smiled. "A girl gets to keep a *few* secrets." She turned to Felix. "I sent them to your tablet."

Felix grabbed his tablet, opened up the file of photos, and passed the device across to Stanley. Then he caught Mabel's eye and gave the signal for a second milkshake.

Stanley swiped through the photos. The smashed glass case. The blood on the floor. The paperweight. Franklin's office in the back. Stanley and Gertie spent a long time examining the two photos of the open safe, then they moved on to the area above Franklin's desk, and finally to one of his file cabinets.

"Wait," Stanley said, leaning closer to the screen. He'd been looking for numbers. Like a combination. Something to explain how Anderson got into that safe so fast. "Look, posted to Franklin's bulletin board above his desk. There's a fraction—3/8. And what's this word next to it?"

Gertie squinted. "That's some bad handwriting. But it looks like . . . 'chin.' Yeah, 'chin.'"

"Chin? What is 'chin 3/8' supposed to mean?"

Felix rubbed his hand through his curly hair. "Beats me. Maybe Old Man Franklin is weird and likes to measure parts of his face?"

Gertie rolled her eyes. "More likely, it means nothing."

Stanley shook his head in frustration. "But numbers always mean *some*thing."

Mabel set a tray down on their table. "Three waters and a Mondo-sized chocolate milkshake with the works. That's your tenth this week, Felix, so it's on the house."

"Thanks, Mabel. You're the mother I never had."

Mabel shrugged. "I'll be sure to let your mother know that when we get together for bowling tonight."

"Aunt, then?" Felix shouted at her as she headed back to the kitchen. "Fairy godmother, perhaps?"

Charlotte sat back down. "What did I miss?"

"Felix is a pig," Gertie said, "and Stanley is frustrated."

"So, in other words, situation normal?"

"Pretty much."

Stanley balled up his napkin, threw it on the table, and stood. "I gotta go."

"Why?" Charlotte asked.

"None of this is fitting together, and I need to go someplace quiet where I can think."

Charlotte smiled at him. "So, like I said, situation normal."

CHAPTER SEVEN

THE WRONG GUY

Stanley left. He left, and he thought. He thought all that night. And all the next day at school, when he should have been paying attention to his teachers, he was still thinking.

And yet, he hadn't solved a single problem.

It would have been next to impossible for Mr. Anderson to guess the right combination to the safe. Mr. Franklin confirmed that he never gave Mr. Anderson the combination. That left only one option. Anderson was some kind of professional safe-cracking thief. But if Anderson really was a pro, why be so dumb as to commit the crime in broad daylight in front of witnesses?

And then there was the timeline. It didn't work. No way Anderson could do everything Franklin and Blump said he did and get out to the roadblock driving less than a hundred miles per hour.

Speaking of Blump, it was awfully curious how much her business had been profiting from Mr. Franklin's misfortune.

And then there was poor Mr. Franklin himself. Something about that hospital visit bothered Stanley. He just didn't know what.

It was during geometry class when an image popped into Stanley's head. Mr. Franklin, bent over slightly to allow the nurse to change his bandages. Stanley had seen the top of Franklin's head. Bald. With stitches running down the center. The nurse had said Franklin was lucky, that it was an especially clean wound. No—that's not *exactly* what she said.

But what *had* she said?

Stanley caught up to Charlotte as they were leaving school that day. "Hey, Charlotte," he hollered. "Think very carefully. In the hospital room, the nurse said something about Franklin's head injury. Can you remember exactly *what* she said?"

"Is this important?" she asked.

Stanley glared at her.

"Fine." Charlotte closed her eyes, took a couple of deep breaths, then opened her eyes and blinked quickly three times.

"*'I still can't believe how straight this cut is. Cleanest head injury I've seen in my 17 years as a nurse, I can tell you that.'*"

"You're sure those were the nurse's exact words?" Stanley asked.

Charlotte folded her arms.

"Of course you're sure." Stanley smiled.

"What's this all about?" Charlotte asked.

"I've got an errand to run."

"You're not going to tell me?"

He jumped on his bike and shook his head. "Don't want to jinx it."

An hour later, Stanley walked out of the emergency room with his answer. He checked his phone and saw that he had missed five calls from Felix.

"Where you been, dude?" Felix asked when Stanley called him back.

"Just putting the puzzle together. I can't wait to tell you what I learned about Mr. Franklin."

Stanley heard Gertie's voice. Felix had put him on speaker. "That's why we're calling you, Stanley. Chief Abrams is about to start a press conference. They've made a major breakthrough in the case, so get down to the courthouse now!"

Stanley ended the call and hopped on his bike. Five minutes later he was running up to the courthouse, where a large crowd had gathered. Cameras were rolling, and Chief Abrams was at the top of the steps, adjusting the microphone. Stanley found his friends just as Abrams began to talk.

"Where were you?" Charlotte whispered.

"The hospital. Remember what Mr. Franklin's nurse said about his cut? Something about that seemed weird to me. I mean, how do you get clobbered on the head by a jagged paperweight and get such a clean and straight cut? So, I talked to the emergency room doctor who took care of Mr. Franklin, and you know what she told me?"

Charlotte leaned in. "What?"

"Well, nothing at first. Apparently, there are laws against telling random kids about people's medical records. But I got what I wanted out of her anyway. I told her a paperweight caused the wound, and that surprised her so much that she started murmuring all these things about the cut being perfect, no jagged edges, no tearing. Really easy to sew back together. She apparently forgot all about those laws and told me she had figured a razor blade caused it, not something like a paperweight."

Felix leaned in. "So, you're saying Anderson cut the top of Franklin's head with a razor blade?"

Stanley shook his head. "No. Not Anderson. I'd bet anything Mr. Franklin cut *himself,* and I think—"

"Shhhh," Gertie said. "Abrams is getting to the good part."

"And after all of the dedicated police work from my office," Abrams was saying, "I am happy to report that we have made a major breakthrough in the case. I can now tell you without a shadow of a doubt that Christopher Anderson is indeed guilty."

"What?" Stanley said a little too loudly. "But there's no way Anderson did this!"

"Cool it, Stanley," Charlotte whispered.

But Stanley wasn't listening. He was wiggling through the crowd, making his way to the front.

Abrams continued. "And I'm sure in a very short while, we will have the Claymore Diamond back in our possession."

"No, you won't!" Stanley shouted.

Abrams stopped abruptly and looked down at Stanley.

Officer Evans shuffled uncomfortably on the chief's right. "Stanley?" he said.

"Hi, Officer Evans. Hi, Chief Abrams. I'm sorry to tell you this, but you've got the wrong guy."

Abrams leaned back and exchanged a confused look with Evans. Then he put a hand over the microphone and peered down.

"I don't know what you think you're doing, young man, but you're interrupting a very important—"

"There is no way Mr. Anderson did this."

"Oh, really?"

"Yes, really. For one thing, the timeline for the crime is all wrong."

"The timeline?"

"Yes, the timeline. For Anderson to argue with Mr. Franklin at 5:55 and steal the diamond, then make it out to your roadblock by 6:21, he would had to have traveled 100 miles per hour. I don't think your officers reported Anderson traveling at a high rate of speed when they stopped him."

Abrams ran his tongue along his bottom lip. "And just how do you know so much about this case?"

Stanley was all of a sudden very much aware of the crowd staring at him. Sweat pooled on his forehead and his throat tightened.

"Um, my friends and I . . . we've been investigating the crime on our own."

Chief Abrams let out a big belly laugh, then leaned over the podium and glared at Stanley. "Exactly how old are you, son?"

Stanley swallowed. "Twelve."

Abrams straightened up and clapped his hands together. "Well, that's just fantastic." He turned to Evans. "You hear that, Bobby? Looks like Ravensburg doesn't even need a police force anymore. We can just let 12-year-old kids solve all the crimes." He laughed again, then turned his glare back on

Stanley. "So according to your investigation, the timeline doesn't work?"

Stanley felt a tug on his arm. He turned. Charlotte was shaking her head back and forth. Gertie and Felix were right behind her. "Don't do it, Stanley."

He spun back toward the podium. "That's right, Chief. The math doesn't work. Mrs. Blump said Anderson went into Franklin's at 5:55. You'll find there's almost no way he could have made it out to your roadblock by 6:21."

The audience had gone dead quiet, and every eye in the crowd was fixed on Chief Abrams, waiting for his response. He looked from the crowd to the TV cameras. Then he grabbed the podium and looked right at Stanley.

"For your information, young man, *we* can do math too. Yes, the timeline, as you call it, did not fit Mrs. Blump's original statement. But maybe, just maybe, since we are the actual police force, maybe we know some things you don't. And we know that

there is no timeline problem because Mr. Anderson actually went into Franklin's Jewelry Store closer to 5:40 p.m."

Stanley was stunned.

"You mean Mrs. Blump *lied?*" Felix yelled.

"Her attorney has used the word 'misremembered,'" the chief replied. "Upon further questioning, she told us the *real* time. Apparently, after hearing the glass shatter, Mrs. Blump hid behind her counter for fifteen minutes before checking on

Mr. Franklin. She was embarrassed about it. But honestly, who can blame her? Christopher Anderson is, after all, a violent criminal."

Stanley still wasn't convinced. "I'm telling you, Chief Abrams, Christopher Anderson isn't the criminal. So, what if the timeline isn't a problem? Why would Anderson be so foolish as to break into Franklin's in broad daylight in front of witnesses?"

"Look, kid, I've had about enough of this. You said foolish, and I'll take it one step further. Christopher Anderson isn't just a *foolish* criminal. He is a *ruthless* criminal with a record a mile long. He's been in and out of different criminal organizations since he was a kid. And, because we are the *real* police, we know he's been going into Franklin's every month for half a year in order to extort money from that poor old man. God bless Mr. Franklin, but he was too frightened to ever tell us. And when Mr. Franklin finally stood up to that madman, Anderson hit him. Hard. That punk saw his opportunity, smashed the display case, used his safe-cracking expertise, and ran out of there with the diamonds. You're right about one thing, kid. This was a very foolish move by a dangerous criminal."

Officer Evans had come down from the podium. He kneeled in front of Stanley. "Stanley, I told you to let the pros handle this, and I was serious. It's time for you to go home and let us take things from here."

Stanley shook his head. "But Mr. Franklin. His head. The clean cut. How do you explain—?"

Abrams pounded on the podium. "You have hit my last nerve and ruined my press conference." He held up a piece of paper. "Before you so rudely interrupted me, I was about to announce that not one hour ago, Christopher Anderson signed his confession."

Stanley's heart nearly stopped. "His *confession?*"

"Yes. Anderson confessed to absolutely everything we charged him with, and now, with his cooperation, hopefully we can find the Claymore Diamond and restore it to its rightful owner."

Stanley spun around. The crowd looked at him as if they expected him to say something. But he had nothing.

Officer Evans put a hand on his shoulder.

"Like I said, Stanley—time to go home."

CHAPTER EIGHT
STANLEY ROBINSON CARUSOE

Felix ran his hands through his hair. "I really thought we were on to something."

The mood in the tree house hadn't been this low since the previous year's talent show, when the four of them recited pi to the two-hundredth place—yet lost to Polly and the English Club's rap remix of the *Romeo and Juliet* window scene. Stanley let out a long sigh. "Well, I guess it's all over. Numbers may not lie, but *I* was wrong about everything."

Charlotte punched him.

"Hey!" he said. "I'm not Felix."

"That's my point. You're *not* Felix. You're Stanley. Stanley Robinson Carusoe. And you're never wrong. Well, your taste in movies is pretty terrible. And you can't dress to save your life."

Gertie sat up. "And you did think Molly Boon liked you that one time, which of course was preposterous."

Felix raised his hand. "And you don't even think Batman is real."

Charlotte put a hand on Stanley's shoulder. "So, I guess sometimes you *are* wrong. But when it comes to stuff like this—math, puzzles, mysteries, and your funny feelings? If you think this doesn't add up, then it doesn't add up."

Stanley looked around the clubhouse. Gertie nodded her head. Felix started grinning. "This is like the part in *Super Friends* when the Wonder Twins yell 'Wonder Twins, activate!' Right?"

Charlotte shook her head and raised her fist. "Remember. Cartoons are weird."

Felix inched back and held up his hands. "Okay, it's like the time in *Rocky II* when Mick yells, 'What are we waiting for?'"

Charlotte smiled. "Much better."

"Well, Carusoe," Gertie said, "what are we waiting for?"

Stanley took a deep breath. "You guys really think I'm right about this kind of stuff?"

His three friends nodded in unison.

"But I just embarrassed us in front of the entire town."

Felix whacked him on the back. "Don't worry about that. The three of us blended into the crowd, so you mostly embarrassed yourself."

"Wow. Thanks."

"I've got a question," Charlotte said. "Is there anything that still doesn't make sense to you?"

Stanley considered. "Well, I keep coming back to Mr. Franklin's cut. I'm telling you, he cut his own head, and I can't think of any reason why he'd do that unless he wanted to frame Mr. Anderson for the crime. But I also know that sounds crazy, seeing as how Anderson just confessed to the whole thing."

Charlotte smiled. "Fortunately, Stanley, you're the least crazy person I know."

"Agreed," Gertie said. She stepped over to the whiteboard and picked up a dry erase marker.

"Which means we need to look at everything in this case like it's new. Where do we start?"

Stanley chewed on his lip. "I guess we start with the numbers. Gertie, get ready to write. Felix, take out your tablet. And Charlotte, we need that memory of yours. I want you to remember every number we've encountered in our investigation. We need to understand how they all fit together."

Charlotte shut her eyes, took a couple of deep breaths, and started to blink. Then she called out numbers. Gertie wrote them down furiously. Then Felix and Stanley tried to see how the numbers fit into the overall puzzle.

They examined each number like they were seeing it for the first time, working it into the picture of how the Claymore Diamond was stolen. But by the time Charlotte had listed almost all of the numbers, the mystery was still as cloudy as ever.

Then she held up her finger.

"I've got one more. 'V chin 3/8.'"

Stanley and Gertie looked at each other.

"You mean 'chin 3/8,' right?" Felix asked.

Charlotte closed her eyes again and shook her head. "Nope. I'm looking at it right now. From one of the photos Gertie took inside Franklin's office. Little scrap of paper, terrible handwriting. I see a 'v' followed by the word 'chin' followed by the fraction '3/8.'"

"Wait a second," Stanley said. "We looked at those pictures at Mabel's. Charlotte, you weren't even there. You were in the bathroom."

"Oh, yeah, I forgot to tell you. I can see through walls now." She laughed. "Just kidding. I looked through Felix's pictures after you left."

"Felix, we need another look at that photo," Stanley said.

Felix pulled up the picture in question and zoomed in. "Well, I'll be. Charlotte's right."

"Of *course* I'm right."

They crowded around Felix's tablet, and sure enough, Stanley could see a small "v" just to the left of the word "chin."

He popped up and began pacing. "V chin 3/8, v chin 3/8. How does this help us? I didn't understand what 'chin 3/8' meant, and I *definitely* don't understand what 'v chin 3/8' means."

Gertie was staring at the photo. "Hmmm. We missed the 'v' before, so what if we're missing other letters too? See, right where the 'v' is, the paper appears to be cut off. What if it's not just 'v chin'? What if there's more to it?" Gertie turned to Felix. "Run a search for words with 'v chin' in them."

"Got it. Okay, um . . . sorry. No words with 'v chin' in them, but—wait a minute, I do know a *name* with 'v chin' in it."

"A name?" Stanley said.

Felix jumped to his feet. "And what a name it is!" He cupped his hands and yelled in an announcer's voice. "And in this corner . . . the heavyweight champion of the world . . . Vladimir Leeeeeeeeevchin!"

"Wait," Stanley said. "Vladimir Levchin, the boxer?"

Felix shrugged. "If you paid more attention to commercials, you'd know all about him. He's got the big title match coming up on *Saturday, Saturday, Saturday!*"

"That could be it," Charlotte said. "'V chin' might be the last five letters in Vladimir Levchin. But then, what about 3/8? What's *that* mean?"

Stanley stared at the whiteboard, where Gertie had now written *Levchin 3/8*.

And that's when it hit him.

CHAPTER NINE

AN ODDS SOLUTION

"It's not a measurement!" Stanley said. "It's not even the fraction three-eighths. It's a *ratio!* As in three to eight. Levchin three to eight! Those are odds!"

"*Very* odd," Gertie agreed.

"No," Stanley said. He was moving about excitedly now. "*Betting* odds. Football. Horse racing. Boxing. There's a ton of gambling that goes on in those sports, and each sport has different ways they handle the betting. For a gambler to make three dollars betting on Levchin to win the bout, that gambler has to bet eight dollars. Spend eight dollars to make three dollars."

"That doesn't sound like a very good bet," Gertie said.

Stanley shrugged. "Depends. The payout may not be very good, but if Levchin is the champion, he must win most of his bouts."

Gertie wrinkled her nose. "But if Levchin wins most of his bouts, why would anyone ever bet on his opponent?"

"Because," Stanley said, "the odds for his opponent will have a better payout. Meaning a gambler will spend less money to make more money. It's how you attract bets to the other side of the bet."

Gertie shook her head. "How do you know all of this?"

Stanley smiled. "Because it's math."

"Okay," Felix said. "Let's say you're right. How does that help us?"

"My guess is that most people don't keep hand-written betting odds lying around," Stanley said.

Charlotte's eyes widened. "I think I get what you're saying," she said. "Mr. Franklin is a gambler."

"Yep." Stanley nodded. "Mr. Franklin is a gambler. And just for a moment, let's assume he's a big-time gambler."

"Okay," Gertie said. "I'm intrigued. Where is this going?"

"Well, gambling isn't exactly the most stable form of income. Sometimes you win, sometimes you lose. And sometimes you lose *big*."

Gertie pointed her pencil at Stanley. "And what if Mr. Franklin lost big?"

"Exactly," Stanley said. "What if he lost *so* big that he needed to steal the Claymore Diamond just to pay off his debts?"

Felix shook his head. "Maybe I've had too many Mondo-sized shakes, but my brain isn't following this. Why would Franklin steal the Claymore Diamond if he already owns it? Why not just sell it and pay off his debt?"

The four friends sat in silence mulling it over.

"Felix is right," Stanley said at last.

"I am?"

"Yes. If Franklin owed $100,000, all he would have to do is sell the Claymore Diamond in order to clear up his debt. But what if he owed *more* than $100,000? What if he owed so much that he needed to sell the diamond *and* collect the insurance money?"

Charlotte folded her arms and leaned back. "Too bad we can't get a look at his bank account."

"Yeah," Stanley said. "Too bad." His eyes suddenly grew wide. "Wait a second—maybe we can."

"Take a look at his bank account?" Charlotte said.

"Not his bank account, but the next best thing—his tax returns. If I've learned anything from doing people's taxes, it's that taxes are the windows into what's really going on in someone's life."

"But how do we access someone's tax returns?" Gertie asked. "I thought those were private."

Stanley shrugged. "Normally they are. Unless someone voluntarily discloses them. And it just so happens that most of the businesses on Main Street have done just that. Remember when Main Street went through that big renovation?"

Felix's eyes widened. "The Make Main Street Beautiful project."

"Exactly," Stanley said. "The project offered grants to improve the businesses along Main Street. But there was a catch. You had to make your tax returns public for five years so the program and the public could track the economic impact of the improvements. All the returns are available on the project's website. Felix?"

"I'm one step ahead of you. Bringing up the website now. Just a second and . . . boom, Franklin's Jewelry Store. Got it!"

"Already?" Gertie said.

"I'm not just a pretty face who likes milkshakes, okay?" Felix licked his lips. "I've got the last three years of tax returns for Franklin's Jewelry Store. What are we looking for?"

"I'm not sure," Stanley said. He squeezed in next to Felix and tapped on the screen. "But numbers have a way of telling their own story."

Gertie squinted. "Looks like Franklin is busiest during the winter and slowest during the summer."

"That makes sense," Charlotte said. "Christmas and Valentine's Day would be the busiest times of the year for buying jewelry, wouldn't they?"

"Yeah, they would," Stanley said. "And it looks like he does a steady business from year to year." He adjusted his glasses. "Wait a second. Right there. All of a sudden, six months ago, things changed. See, his income suddenly went way down. After making a consistent profit for two and a half years, Franklin started to lose money."

"Stanley, you're right. And not just a little bit of money." Gertie furiously wrote down some figures. "Listen to this. Over the last six months, Franklin lost $195,000."

"Excuse me?" Stanley said.

"You heard me. One hundred and ninety-five thousand big ones."

"Wow, Stanley," Felix said. "You really were right. But I don't get it. If Franklin was losing money gambling, what would that have to do with his business?"

Stanley was smiling. "It actually makes perfect sense. The less money your business makes, the less you pay in taxes. Franklin owed so much that he was probably trying to save on taxes by cooking the books to show his business was losing money."

Gertie surveyed the whiteboard. "All of this is starting to fit together. Well, except for this." She drew a circle around Christopher Anderson's name. "I still don't understand where he fits in."

Stanley tapped on the whiteboard, then snapped his fingers. "I'll bet you anything I know what happened. Anderson went to Franklin's, and for some reason, he and the old man got into an argument. The fight gave Franklin a bright idea about how to pay his gambling debts. As soon as Anderson left, Franklin opened the safe and hid the Claymore Diamond. Then he cracked the display cases and stole a few more diamonds. Then he cut his own head, and broke the front window to get Mrs. Blump's attention. Finally, he lay down on the floor, planted the paperweight at his side, and waited. At some point, Blump called 911, the cops found Franklin lying in a pool of his own blood, and Franklin told his story about Christopher Anderson. Case closed."

Stanley was almost out of breath. The others looked at him, eyes wide, mouths open.

"And that means," Stanley continued, "unless we find that diamond before Mr. Franklin sells it, Mr.

Anderson will go to jail for a crime he didn't commit."

Charlotte shrugged. "Still doesn't explain why Anderson confessed."

"No, it doesn't," Stanley agreed. "I haven't figured that part out yet. But we're running out of time, and we need to find that diamond. Any ideas where it might be?"

"The cops have been through Franklin's store and office with a fine-tooth comb," Felix said. "No way it's there."

"Which means he had to take it with him when he went to the hospital!" Stanley said. "And luckily, Charlotte 'took pictures' of his hospital room." He winked at her.

Charlotte winked back, then closed her eyes. She opened them and blinked quickly. "Hat and jacket on the chair near the window. Cup of water on the tray near his bed. Black briefcase on the floor to his left."

Stanley snapped his fingers again. "The briefcase! Remember how he wouldn't let the nurse touch his stuff? He must have hidden the Claymore Diamond in his briefcase, taken it to the hospital, and then—"

"He took it home!" Gertie shouted.

Stanley nodded. "And now he'll let Anderson take the fall for the crime while he files the insurance claim and finds a buyer for that diamond on the black market."

Gertie hit her hand with her fist. "That rotten, no-good . . . I say we go to his house, bust his door down, and give Old Man Franklin what's coming to him. And by *we,* I mean Charlotte, of course."

"I don't think beating up an old guy is going to help our credibility with Chief Abrams," Charlotte said.

Stanley nodded. "What we need is proof."

Felix jumped out of his seat. "I have it!"

"Have what?" Gertie said.

"I know what to do. I *actually know* what we need to do." Felix sat back down, folded his hands behind his head, and smiled.

"Out with it, or I pummel you," Charlotte said.

"Fair enough. We don't need violence—not against Mr. Franklin, and certainly not against me. What we need is a good old-fashioned stakeout, a little bluff, and lots and *lots* of Scooby snacks."

CHAPTER TEN
STAKEOUT

On any other Monday in September, a late-night excursion would have been difficult. But thanks to teacher in-services the following day, the four friends found themselves high up in a large oak tree about 20 yards from Mr. Franklin's house just after dark. Felix had his Spynoculars trained on the living room window, watching Franklin, who sat in his recliner in front of the TV.

"The old Franklin place," Felix said wistfully from a branch near the top. "I can't believe the old coot was the bad guy after all, even if every *Scooby-Doo* episode *does* end that way."

"Use the hunting binoculars, Felix," Charlotte ordered from just below him. She looked to her left. "Stanley, you really think this will work?"

"Only one way to find out." He looked to a branch just below him. "Gertie, make the call. And remember to rhyme."

Gertie glared up at Stanley, then took out her cell phone, turned on the speaker, and dialed Mr. Franklin's number.

A few seconds later, Felix held his thumb up in the air. "Franklin is reaching for the phone," he whispered.

"Arnold Franklin speaking. May I help you?"

"Mr. Franklin," Gertie began, "this is Stella Burger with Channel 12 Action News." Gertie's imitation was perfect.

"Sorry, miss, but I've already told my story to the press, and tonight I just want to—"

"You misunderstand, Mr. Franklin. There's been a new development in your case, and I wanted to get your comment."

"A new development?" Mr. Franklin said.

"He just straightened up in his chair," Felix whispered. "Looks nervous."

"Yes," Gertie said. "We just received a tip from our source down at the courthouse that Judge Lewis has signed a search warrant for the police to go through your car and your house."

"What?" the old jeweler squealed.

"And before the police get there, we wanted to know if you had any idea what they hope to find."

"Uh, I have no idea, but this is outrageous. I've got to go."

Gertie smiled. "If you change your mind, do call back. And remember, *12 is Swell!*"

"Franklin just slammed the phone down," Felix reported. "Standing up, now pacing back and forth across the living room. Oscar-winning performance, Gertie—I think he bought it."

"Okay, Charlotte," Stanley said. "Get that camera ready. Who knows what Franklin will do."

Charlotte took out a high-resolution camera with a telescopic lens and night vision display and focused it on the window.

Felix kept his binoculars trained on Franklin's house as well. "Okay, guys, Franklin's spooked, running upstairs. I've lost him, no visual. Repeat,

no visual. No, wait—he's back, running down the stairs. He's grabbing a black coat out of the closet. Now a hat. Heading for the door."

"Charlotte, start taking pictures as soon as he hits the door," Stanley said.

Franklin came outside, walked straight to his unattached garage, and opened the door. He came back out with a shovel.

"You getting all this, Charlotte?" Stanley asked in a hoarse whisper.

"Every bit. Now be quiet and let me concentrate."

Franklin took out his shovel and began to dig.

After a few minutes, the old man pulled something out of his black coat, dropped it into the hole, and covered it with dirt. Then he hustled to the garage, put the shovel away, shut the door, and went back into his house.

"Did you guys see that?" Felix said excitedly. "We meddling kids just foiled his sinister plot!"

"There's only one way to be sure," Stanley said.

"We gonna dig it up?" Charlotte asked.

"Not us." Stanley dialed a number on his phone, put it on speaker, and let it ring.

"Officer Bobby Evans," a voice answered.

"Hi, Officer Evans. It's Stanley Carusoe."

"Am I to assume you're calling to apologize for that performance today?"

"Um, sort of. I would like to make up for my mistake."

"At least you're willing to admit it, Stanley. That's the first step."

"No, I meant that there's been a new development in the Franklin case that can't wait until morning."

Evans growled through the phone. "Stanley, I think maybe I need to sit down with your parents and explain the hazards of interfering with police business."

"That conversation is going to have to wait. I'm afraid we're sort of up a tree right now."

After a long pause, Evans said, "Where are you kids?"

Felix grinned. "Like Stanley said, we're up a tr—"

Gertie socked him in the shoulder.

"We're outside Mr. Franklin's house," Stanley said. He gave Evans the address.

Evans let out a heavy sigh. Then, "Stay right there. I'm coming to get you."

Six minutes later, Stanley and Charlotte waved Evans down a block from Franklin's house.

He got out of the car. "You're wearing camo paint?"

"Felix's idea," Charlotte explained. "We're all wearing it. Scarves, too."

"Where *is* Felix? And Gertie, for that matter?" Evans asked.

Stanley pointed a thumb over his shoulder. "They're keeping an eye on Mr. Franklin."

And then, before Evans could remind them how much trouble they were in, Charlotte held up the digital camera for him to see. She clicked through the photos one by one. "These are pictures of Mr. Franklin's house. In this picture, you see him leaving his house. Here you see him grabbing a shovel from his garage. Here you see him digging a hole in his backyard. And here you see him burying something."

She and Stanley looked up at the young officer, expecting praise.

"Do you have any idea how much trouble the four of you are in?"

"But we have reason to believe that what he buried is the Claymore Diamond," Stanley explained.

Evans rolled his eyes. "And I assume you have some actual *proof* for this ridiculous assertion?"

"If you're willing to listen," Stanley said, "really *listen,* then yes, I'll tell you everything I know."

Evans practically chewed through his lip. Then finally he relaxed and nodded. "Make it fast."

And Stanley did. He and Charlotte laid out exactly what they thought Franklin did, why he did it, and what led them to believe it. By the end of it all, Evans was scratching his chin. He looked at the pictures again—more intensely this time. Then he took out his phone and called Chief Abrams. He explained that they needed a search warrant—and fast.

It wasn't long before Chief Abrams arrived at the Franklin house with a search warrant. But not to search Franklin's house. To search his *yard*. Stanley and his friends stood back and watched as Evans went to the exact spot in the photo where they'd seen Mr. Franklin bury something. It took Evans only three minutes of digging before he unearthed a black velvet bag. He pulled the bag from the hole and handed it to Chief Abrams.

Chief Abrams reached into the bag—and pulled out the biggest and most beautiful diamond any of them had ever seen.

The case of the Claymore Diamond was solved.

Well, almost.

CHAPTER ELEVEN
ONE LAST PROBLEM

In the weeks that followed, media outlets scrambled to get the first interview with the recently released Christopher Anderson. But Anderson turned down the big national news outlets in favor of a local anchor, Dina Bell from Channel 8 News. To outsiders, this was a curious decision, but to the Ravensburg viewing public, the choice of Stella Burger's biggest rival was eminently logical.

Stanley, Charlotte, Gertie, and Felix watched the interview on the TV in the tree house.

On screen, Chris Anderson was seated on a comfortable couch, his arm around a very pretty woman. Both were facing Dina Bell.

Dina leaned in for her first question. "So, Chris, why don't you introduce the lovely lady sitting next to you?"

Anderson blushed and said, "This is Melanie Brewster. And as of last night, she is my fiancée."

"Congratulations to you both," Dina said. "That's wonderful news. And you've had quite a bit of news lately, haven't you?"

"That I have." Anderson smiled.

Dina's expression turned serious. "And it's that other news that our viewers are interested in. Let's start with the big question, Chris. Why did you plead guilty to a crime you did not commit?"

It was Melanie who answered. "It was because of me," she said. "I didn't know it, but Chris was going to propose to me the day he was arrested. He'd been paying off an engagement ring for six months. When he went in to make the final payment, Arnold Franklin tried to blackmail him for more money. The police say that Franklin needed a lot of money quickly for gambling debts. Anyway, Franklin had fabricated all sorts of evidence that supposedly proved Chris was involved in extorting money from him. None of it was true, but Franklin wanted $200,000 dollars to destroy the evidence. When Chris told him he didn't have that kind of money, Franklin told him to get ahold of his old crime buddies to help him come up with the cash. And since Franklin knew about the engagement ring, he figured Chris would do just about anything to try to stay out of jail."

Dina shook her head. "But Chris, why didn't you just go to the police with the fake evidence Franklin had against you?"

"Well . . ." Anderson looked uncomfortable. "When I was a teenager, I got into quite a bit of trouble. I've cleaned up my act now, but I guess I didn't think the police would believe my word over Mr. Franklin's."

Melanie jumped in. "And since nobody really knew how serious our relationship had grown, Chris didn't want to risk people knowing about us. He was afraid it would cause me a lot of problems, so he couldn't explain to anyone why he was at Franklin's in the first place. He told me that since he was going to go to jail either way, he'd try to plead guilty to stealing the Claymore and hope to get a lesser sentence."

Dina nodded in understanding. "So *you*, Chris, were the one Sheila Blump heard say, 'You're a liar and a thief, and you'll never get away with this'?"

"That's right," Anderson said. "I tried to leave the store then, but Mr. Franklin grabbed me. We crashed into the display case. I was so upset, I ran outta there, hopped in my car, and drove off. I don't even know where I was going. I just had to get away and think. Before I knew it, the cops had pulled me over and were reading me my rights."

"So, Mr. Franklin stole the Claymore Diamond himself and framed you for the crime?"

Anderson nodded.

Dina shook her head, then smiled mischievously. "And you left Main Street without picking up your truffles?"

Melanie laughed. "He'd been bringing them to me the 15th of every month for six months. Now I know why. He told me the last one was supposed to be twice as big, and he was going to have Mrs. Blump put the ring in the box before she wrapped it."

The view switched to a headshot of Dina. "You've heard it from their own mouths, Ravensburg. Tune into Channel 8, where *we* are always breaking news. This has been a special report by me, Dina Bell. Remember, When Channel 8 Investigates, We Get in Your Face!"

Gertie threw her hands in the air. "What is wrong with this town? How hard is it to rhyme? Speaking of which, turn on Channel 12. It's just about time."

Felix aimed the remote at the TV and fired twice. Chief Abrams's large figure took up the entire screen. He was holding a final press conference on the Claymore Diamond affair.

Abrams explained that Arnold Franklin was being charged on multiple counts of felony fraud, grand larceny, and tax evasion. He then went on to briefly outline the facts of the case, and he attested to the complete innocence of Christopher Anderson. The chief looked embarrassed about his earlier missteps, but at the same time, he attempted to hint that he knew Anderson was innocent all along.

When he opened the floor for questions, a very dejected-looking Stella Burger asked how the department finally figured out the truth. As per Stanley's wishes, Chief Abrams explained that the investigation had been aided by a group calling themselves "The Math Inspectors."

Then, as final payment for their help, Chief Abrams looked directly into the camera and said, "After all, math really is a wonderful subject. Come to think of it, of all possible intellectual pursuits, the most important, the one at the top, is, without a doubt, math." He pointed at the camera and bellowed, "You got that, Polly?"

Stanley, Charlotte, Gertie, and Felix roared with approval.

When Charlotte finally finished laughing, she took another bite of a cupcake. "Wow, Felix, this chocolate cupcake is great. Tell your mom thanks!"

"My mom's chocolate supreme cupcake. Her specialty," Felix said.

Felix reached for the big cupcake he had saved for himself. But instead of a cupcake, all he found was a plate full of crumbs. He panicked, looked around as Stanley and Gertie ate their cupcakes, then rushed to the window. Just below, strutting across the yard, was a fluffy white cat with dark crumbs all over his face.

"Buckets!" he yelled.

While Felix scrambled down the rope and ran after his cat, Stanley Robinson Carusoe leaned toward Gertie and whispered, "Do you think Felix will ever figure out that you've been teaching Buckets how to steal his food?"

Gertie's eyes grew wide. "How did you know?"

Stanley shrugged. "Like you guys told me, I'm pretty good at mysteries."

CHAPTER TWELVE
MEANWHILE

A heavy door opened into a small white room, and the guard pointed at a chair pulled up to the visitors' window. Prisoner 37066 sat down. The door closed, and the prisoner was left all alone.

The prisoner looked through the thick glass at the visitors' area. Two phones, one on either side of the glass, allowed communication between prisoner and visitor. Prisoner 37066 wondered who in the world was coming to visit.

For several long minutes, nothing happened. Nobody came. Nobody sat down.

Then the phone rang.

It rang seven times before the prisoner picked it up. "Who—who is this?"

"Maybe you haven't heard," said a smooth voice, "but I do not like waiting."

The prisoner almost dropped the phone. "Are you the—?"

"Yes, I am."

"I'm really, really sorry about not getting you your money. But it's not my fault. You don't know what happened. Those kids, they—"

"I am not interested in excuses," said the calm voice on the other end, the one belonging to the Boss. "Those meddlesome kids got lucky playing at detective work. They are not worthy of my notice. But you . . . well, that is a different story."

"Me?" The prisoner's voice cracked. "I'm in a maximum-security prison for the next ten years. I've lost everything I've ever owned. I've got nothing you want."

"Fortunately for you," said the Boss in an almost cheery voice, "you are wrong. In fact, you have something so valuable that I'm willing not only to forgive your bungling of the diamond affair, but also to arrange a bit of an upgrade in your prison accommodations. Say, to a minimum-security facility. No violence. Plenty of trees."

The prisoner hesitated. "You'd do that?"

"If you give me what I want."

"But what could I possibly have that's worth *that?*"

The Boss laughed quietly. "I'm planning a little party for the lovely town of Ravensburg—something that will make the Claymore Diamond affair seem like child's play. But I confess that a few details in the plan are holding me up. What I need from you is a little . . . inside information. Do we have a deal?"

For the first time in a very, very long time, Prisoner 37066 smiled. "What do you want to know?"

THE END

BONUS MATH PROBLEMS . . .

Do You Have What It Takes

To Be A Math Inspector?

Hey, Gertie here! Stanley asked Felix and me to come up with a few problems to test whether or not you've got what it takes to be a Math Inspector. And as you'd expect, Felix is taking this job quite seriously. In fact, right now he's doing a handstand in the corner of the tree house while sticking cherry Twizzlers up his nose.

So, as usual, it looks like I will have to do all the work myself.

First, I'm going to let you in on a little secret— all detective stories are word problems. You know, those dreaded last few problems of every math assignment? The ones where you'd rather cuddle with a porcupine than have to solve them? Well, get out your magnifying glass because those problems are there to sharpen your *detective* skills! I'm pretty sure the ones in your textbooks are so boring because they let the English Club write them. But we won't let that stop us—we are the *Math Inspectors!*

I've come up with a series of fun detective problems for you to solve. And when you think you've gotten them right, go to our website at www.TheMathInspectors.com to check your answers.

Got it? Good.

Oh, no. It looks like Felix has gotten hold of a bag of Cheetos and some powdered donuts. I'd better get Buckets, and fast! Gertie out.

Word Problem #1 - A girl named Polly Partridge crawls out from under a rock and walks into a store looking to buy witch's brooms for the entire English Club. Witch's brooms are on sale for 10% off the usual price of $15.00, and Polly only has $130.00 to spend. How many brooms can Polly buy with $130.00?

Word Problem #2 – A woman named Stella Burger goes to a camp where they teach people how to properly rhyme. The cost to attend is $12.00 for each half-day, and her boss wants her to attend camp for 9 full days. However, on the 9th day, Stella has to leave halfway through the day to report on the breaking news that a girl from a local English Club has just pulled a muscle in her brain. How much money did Stella spend attending Rhyming Camp?

Hey, dudes, it's Felix! Not sure what happened, but my Cheetos and powdered donuts are missing, and I lost one of the Twizzlers in my nose. Plus, Gertie's getting really angry for some reason, so I thought I'd take over for a little bit.

Word problems? This should be easy. I eat word problems for breakfast. Especially if there's bacon with them. Mmmmm, bacon-covered word problems. Now that's what I'm talking about.

Word Problem #3 – Let's say, hypothetically, that Mrs. Blump challenged me to eat as many of her chocolate truffles as I could in 15 minutes. And let's say that, on average, I can eat 4.7 truffles per minute. How many truffles would I eat in 15 minutes? And, if each truffle cost $1.75, how much money would I spend? And as a bonus, do you think I would end up getting sick right there in the

store or somewhere in the street as I rode my bike home?

It's Gertie, and I'm back! Enough with the food, Felix. It's time to get back to serious word problems. No, the next one is not going to be about Polly, and it's certainly not going to be about tall, goofy-looking redheads. Not even close. Just pay attention and try to follow along.

Word Problem #4 – The annual Biggest Doofus In Ravensburg contest was held, and the race came down to two finalists. A girl named Molly Martridge and a boy named Welix Wervish. Out of the 300 votes cast, 53% were for Mr. Wervish and 47% were for Miss Martridge. How many votes did each candidate get?

Felix here. Ha, Biggest Doofus, that's good. And Welix Wervish. That's a funny name. It's sounds kind of like—

Hey, wait a minute! Gertie, get back here!

To check your answers or to learn more about the Math Inspectors, go to www.TheMathInspectors.com.

Or to find other great books for kids, go to www.BakkenBooks.com.

www.bakkenbooks.com

The mission of Bakken Books is to provide kids
with wholesome books that teach character
lessons, core virtues, and strong moral values.

We strive to provide content that parents can
TRUST and kids will LOVE!

Other Bakken Books Stories

Camping books for kids

Mystery books for kids

Hunting books for kids

Fishing books for kids

Gaming books for kids

www.bakkenbooks.com

Math adventures for kids

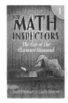

History adventures for kids

Space adventures for kids

Humorous adventures for kids

Racing adventures for kids

ABOUT THE AUTHORS

DANIEL KENNEY

Daniel Kenney and his wife live in Nebraska with their eight children and one very tiny dog. Daniel brings his experience as a high school teacher and a father to the work he does as a children's author. He has published more than thirty-five children's books and strives to write fun and adventurous stories that affirm timeless values such as courage, friendship, and family.

EMILY BOEVER

Emily Boever is a homeschooling mom with eight great kids. She and her husband raise the younger ones of the crew in Omaha, Nebraska. There, Emily splits her time between homemaking, homeschooling, and gawking at pictures of the recently arrived first grandbaby.

Emily has taught high school and college history courses for decades, and in recent years, she has added writing skills and storytelling courses to her online teaching business.

Whenever possible, she enjoys traveling, both to escape the Nebraska winters in favor of the Florida sunshine and to teach her kids about history through firsthand investigation.

Made in the USA
Las Vegas, NV
19 November 2024

12156940R00079